MAY   2018

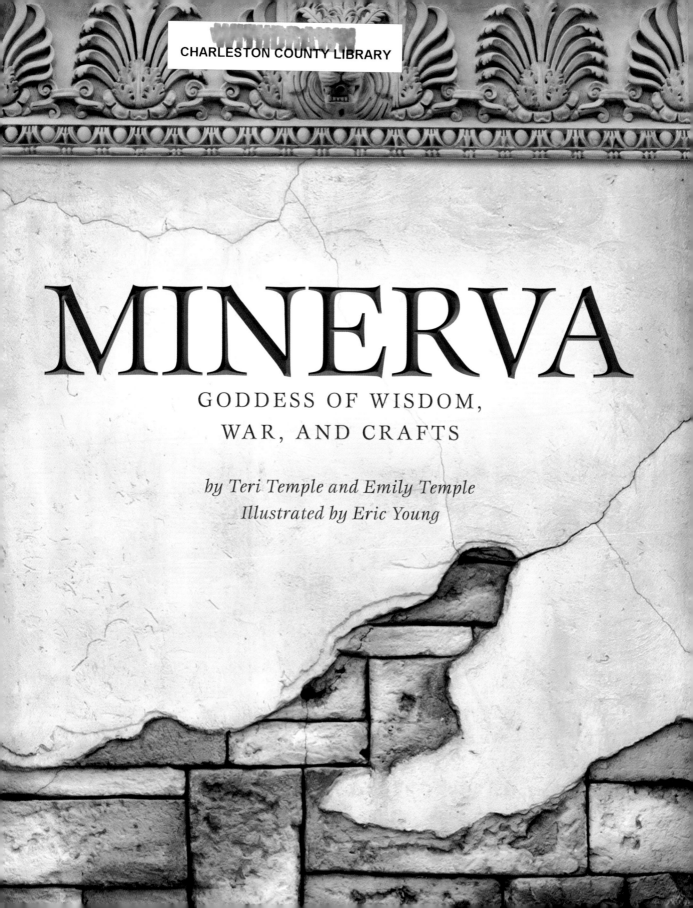

MINERVA

GODDESS OF WISDOM, WAR, AND CRAFTS

by Teri Temple and Emily Temple

Illustrated by Eric Young

Published by The Child's World®
1980 Lookout Drive • Mankato, MN 56003-1705
800-599-READ • www.childsworld.com

ACKNOWLEDGMENTS
The Child's World®: Mary Berendes, Publishing Director
Red Line Editorial: Editorial direction
The Design Lab: Design and production
Design elements ©: Banana Republic Images/Shutterstock Images; Shutterstock Images; Anton Balazh/Shutterstock Images
Photographs ©: Viacheslav Lopatin/Shutterstock Images, 5; Shutterstock Images, 11, 16; Bettmann/Corbis, 15; Pattavikorn Ployprasert/Shutterstock Images, 22; Sergio Bertino/Shutterstock Images, 28

ISBN 9781631437212
LCCN 2014945313

Printed in the United States of America
PA02346

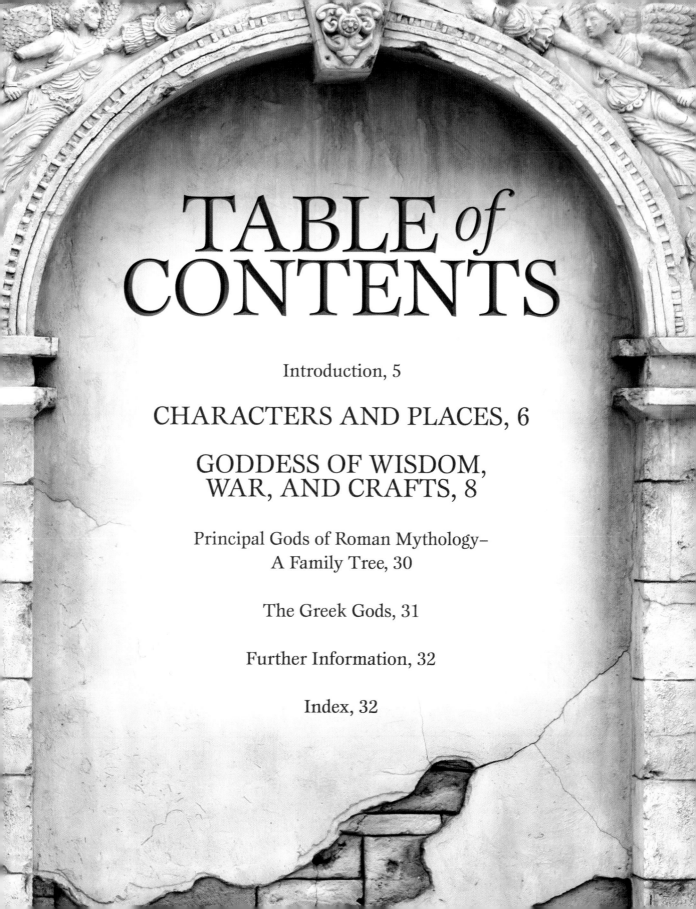

TABLE *of* CONTENTS

INTRODUCTION

In ancient times Romans believed in spirits or gods called numina. In Latin, *numina* means divine will or power. The Romans took part in religious rituals to please the gods. They felt the gods had powers that could make their lives better.

As the Roman government grew more powerful, its armies conquered many neighboring lands. Romans often adopted beliefs from these new cultures. They greatly admired the Greek arts and sciences. Gradually, the Romans combined the Greek myths and religion with their own. These stories shaped and influenced each part of a Roman citizen's daily life. Ancient Roman poets, such as Ovid and Virgil, wrote down these tales of wonder. Their writings became a part of Rome's great history. To the Romans, however, these stories were not just for entertainment. Roman mythology was their key to understanding the world.

ANCIENT ROMAN SOCIETIES
Ancient Roman society was divided into several groups. The patricians were the most powerful and wealthiest group. They often owned land and held power in the government. The plebeians worked for the patricians. Slaves were prisoners of war or children without parents. Some slaves were freed and enjoyed most of the rights of citizens.

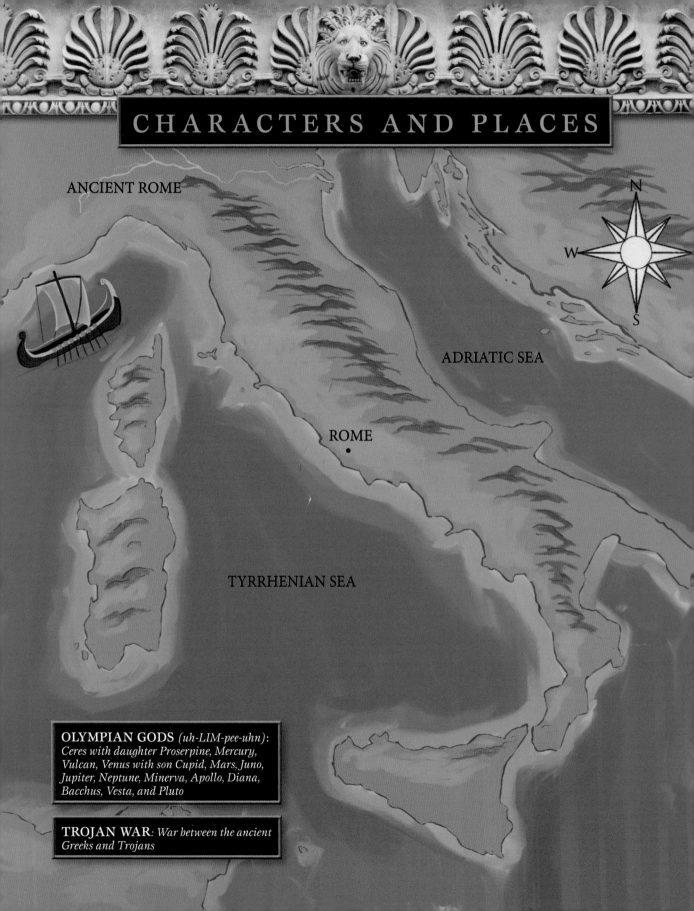

CHARACTERS AND PLACES

ANCIENT ROME

N
W   S

ADRIATIC SEA

ROME

TYRRHENIAN SEA

OLYMPIAN GODS *(uh-LIM-pee-uhn)*:
*Ceres with daughter Proserpine, Mercury,
Vulcan, Venus with son Cupid, Mars, Juno,
Jupiter, Neptune, Minerva, Apollo, Diana,
Bacchus, Vesta, and Pluto*

TROJAN WAR: *War between the ancient
Greeks and Trojans*

ARACHNE *(uh-RAK-nee)*

Woman who challenged Minerva to a weaving contest and was changed into a spider for her presumption

BELLEROPHON *(buh-LER-uh-fon)*

Mythological hero who mounted Pegasus the winged horse

HERCULES *(HUR-kyuh-leez)*

Son of Jupiter; hero of Roman myths

JUPITER *(JOO-pi-ter)*

Supreme ruler of the heavens and of the gods on Mount Olympus; son of Saturn and Ops; married to Juno; father of many gods and heroes

MEDUSA *(muh-DOO-suh)*

Snake-haired creature whose gaze turned men to stone; mother of Pegasus; slayed by Perseus

MINERVA *(mi-NUR-vuh)*

Goddess of wisdom and the arts; daughter of Jupiter

NIKE *(NYE-kee)*

Goddess of victory

ODYSSEUS *(oh-DIS-ee-uhs)*

Hero featured in the epic poems the Illiad *and the* Odyssey

PERSEUS *(PUR-see-uhs)*

Hero who killed Medusa; married to Andromeda

GODDESS OF WISDOM, WAR, AND CRAFTS

In Roman mythology, Minerva was a warrior goddess. She was also the goddess of wisdom, arts, trades, and war. Of all the gods and goddesses, Minerva's birth story is one of the most unique. There are many versions of her story. But the most widely accepted version begins with Jupiter, the king of the gods.

Jupiter's first wife was Metis. She was the Titan goddess of good counsel, advice, and wisdom. Metis served as Jupiter's counselor. Not long after they were married, Metis became pregnant with their first child. Everything seemed perfect. But Terra, Mother Earth, soon warned Jupiter of a prophecy.

Terra told Jupiter that Metis would one day overthrow him. Jupiter knew he couldn't let that happen. But he also did not want to lose Metis's good advice. So he came up with a plan. He tricked Metis into becoming a tiny fly. He then swallowed her up. He foolishly believed his problems were solved.

A few days later, Jupiter began suffering massive headaches. He eventually asked his son Vulcan for help. Vulcan used his ax to split open Jupiter's pounding head. To their great surprise, Minerva sprang from his skull. She was fully grown and dressed in armor. Minerva came into the world with a battle cry.

Minerva's father was the most powerful god. Her mother was the wisest. As a result, Minerva was a perfect blend of power and wisdom. Minerva was the Roman patroness of agriculture. She created the plow and rake. She taught mortals how to yoke oxen so they could pull the plows. She also created the olive tree. Many other inventions in the arts and sciences were credited to her as well, such as the creation of numbers.

Minerva ruled over the arts and crafts men and women practiced. She took part in spinning and weaving. She taught these skills to housewives. Minerva was also a patron of physicians and medicine. The Roman poet Ovid named her the goddess of a thousand works.

ROMAN MEDICINE

Much of Roman medicine came from the Greeks. Formal training for doctors existed in Rome. But anyone could call him or herself a doctor. Doctors often served as surgeons in the army. Roman doctors improved humans' overall understanding of both hygiene and health. Citizens obtained advice from their doctors but still prayed to the gods for good health. The caduceus has come to be known as a symbol for physicians. This staff features wings and two snakes.

Minerva became identified with the Greek warrior goddess Athena. They shared many of the same attributes. Some ancient Romans believed they were the same goddess.

Minerva was beautiful. She had great power and was often considered Jupiter's favorite child. He loved her so much that he gave her his treasured Aegis. The Aegis was his special breastplate. It was so strong, nothing could damage or break it. The Aegis became one of Minerva's greatest pieces of armor.

More often than not, Minerva wore body armor and a helmet. She often carried a shield and a spear. Olives from the olive trees she created symbolized the peace that comes at the end of war. Her sacred animal was the owl. The owl is a symbol of wisdom. It was often seen with Minerva. Minerva became known for her wisdom and justice. Mortals often asked Minerva for her sound judgment and good council.

Although Minerva was worshiped as the goddess of war, she did not look upon war as the other gods of war did. Her beliefs about war conflicted with those of Mars, the other Roman god of war. Mars reveled in a bloody battle. Minerva preferred peace. She represented justice and skill.

Even so, Minerva was a fierce warrior. One of her constant companions on the battlefield was Nike. Nike was the goddess of victory. Minerva led the armies for her state against its enemies in times of war. With Nike at her side, Minerva was sure to win each battle. The goddesses fought together for causes that were just.

ROMAN GOVERNMENT
A senate, two consuls, and an assembly ruled the ancient Roman government. The senate collected taxes. It was made up of wealthy landowners. The consuls controlled Rome. Citizens of Rome elected consuls by a majority vote. Consuls served for one year. Senators selected by the consuls remained members for life. Working-class citizens elected the assembly. The assembly represented the voice of the people.

Minerva also had the job of maintaining the laws. She kept order in the courts. Ancient Romans believed she created the ancient government and laws. When there was a case that divided the votes of the judges equally, Minerva gave the final vote.

When not on the battlefield or settling disputes, Minerva enjoyed music and crafts. She was also a skilled inventor. Minerva created several musical instruments. One was a kind of flute. However, she didn't like the flute. So she threw it aside.

Minerva preferred weaving. She enjoyed crafting beautiful tapestries. These heavy cloths were woven to look like pictures. Once a young woman named Arachne bragged that she wove better than Minerva. Minerva was furious. She challenged Arachne to a contest. Each would weave one tapestry.

Minerva sat at her loom and created a flawless tapestry of the Olympian gods. Arachne's tapestry was also flawless. But it showed only how foolish the gods could be. This disrespect was

THE FLUTE

Ancient Romans believed Minerva invented music and a kind of flute. Juno and Venus laughed at the way Minerva looked when she played it. Minerva sat down beside a pool of water. In her reflection, she saw the way her cheeks puffed out as she played each note. Embarrassed, she cast away her flute. It is said that Marsyas, a satyr, picked it up and played it.

more than Minerva could handle. She ripped the tapestry to shreds. Then she turned Arachne into the first spider. Arachne was forced to spin thread and weave forever.

Minerva found a friend in the hero Odysseus. He was smart, just, and cunning. As the goddess of war, Minerva chose to help Odysseus during the Trojan War. The Trojan War was an epic battle between the Greeks and the Trojans.

Minerva was a brilliant war strategist. She gave the Greeks an idea to help them defeat the Trojans. Minerva knew the Trojans would never refuse a gift from her. So she told Odysseus and the Greeks to send a wooden horse into the city of Troy. The Trojans foolishly opened their gates and accepted the gift. But they did not know what was inside the horse. As soon as the horse entered the city, Greek soldiers leapt out and attacked. They destroyed Troy and ended the Trojan War.

Many of the gods had chosen sides during the Trojan War. Odysseus was thankful for the protection and guidance Minerva had given him. Now he needed her protection even more for his journey home.

The gods who had supported the Trojans wanted to punish Odysseus for defeating them. They created all sorts of problems for him. Odysseus had particularly angered the sea god Neptune when he blinded his son Polyphemus. As he sailed back to his wife and son, Odysseus was held prisoner by the sea nymph Calypso. He finally escaped after seven years, only to endure more storms and shipwrecks Neptune created for him. Minerva didn't want to anger the other gods. She could only offer Odysseus guidance and advice through his dreams.

It took 10 long years, but Odysseus eventually returned home. Minerva had warned him that many noblemen wished to marry his wife. Odysseus had been gone so long that these men and his wife were certain Odysseus had died. Minerva helped disguise Odysseus. When he reached home, he defeated more than 100 men. Odysseus won back his wife and his throne.

Perseus was another hero Minerva favored. Perseus was a son of Jupiter. His mother was a human named Danae. A prophecy told Danae's father that his grandson would one day kill him. So Danae's father cast Danae and baby Perseus into the sea. Perseus had to fight to survive from the very start. When he was grown, he was sent on a mission. He was to collect the head of the Gorgon Medusa.

Medusa had once served as Minerva's attendant. Medusa was very beautiful. She caught the attention of the sea god Neptune. While Medusa was visiting Minerva's temple, Neptune approached Medusa. Medusa was enchanted, and the two fell in love. Minerva found out and was furious. She and Neptune often did not see eye-to-eye. Minerva

THE GORGONS

Medusa was one of the three Gorgon sisters. Each had hissing snakes for hair. Their hideous appearance could turn men to stone. They were the daughters of the sea god Phorcys and the sea monster Ceto. Ancient warriors carved the image of the Gorgons onto armor. They thought the images would terrify their enemies, as well as protect them from evil spells.

did not want Medusa and Neptune together. Minerva
couldn't punish Neptune, so instead she punished
Medusa. She turned Medusa into a hideous creature with
snakes for hair. She also took away Medusa's immortality.

Medusa could turn her enemies to stone with a single look. Obtaining her head seemed impossible. But Minerva wanted Perseus to succeed. Jupiter added his help as well. He sent Mercury, the messenger god, to lend a hand. Together they formulated a plan. With the gods at his side, Perseus was sure he would be victorious.

Perseus traveled to the island of the Gorgons to find Medusa. He took with him Minerva's shiny bronze shield and Mercury's sword. Minerva had given him a plan for when he arrived. She told Perseus to use the shield as a mirror. If he looked at Medusa directly, he would turn to stone. The reflection from the shield allowed him to see Medusa without looking her in the eye.

Perseus shuddered at the sight of the three Gorgons sleeping on the beach. With living snakes for hair, they were surrounded by the stone statues of the men who had come before Perseus. Using the reflection from Minerva's shield as a guide, Perseus beheaded Medusa. He placed the monstrous head in a bag. He gave it to Minerva as thanks. Medusa's head was mounted onto Minerva's breastplate.

Minerva was known for helping other heroes too. One of these was Bellerophon, a son of Neptune. Bellerophon wanted to tame the divine winged horse, Pegasus. Everyone did, but no gods had been able to accomplish the feat. On his own, Bellerophon was unsuccessful. One night while he slept on Minerva's shrine, Minerva appeared in his dream. In the dream, she gave him a starry bridle to use on Pegasus. Much to his surprise, when Bellerophon awoke, he found the bridle lying next to him. The bridle allowed him to easily tame Pegasus, just as Minerva had said.

Ancient legend also claims Minerva helped the hero Hercules three separate times. Hercules was also a son of Jupiter. But his mother was a mortal. Furious about another of Jupiter's affairs, Juno drove Hercules crazy. As a result, he killed his wife and children. As punishment, Hercules was to complete 12 labors. During one of these, Minerva helped him defeat the man-eating Stymphalian birds. She also helped Hercules capture Cerberus, the three-headed dog that protected the gates of the underworld.

Minerva was the goddess of wisdom, the arts, science, trades, and war. With so many things under her watchful eye, nearly everyone in ancient Rome loved and worshiped Minerva. The Temple of Minerva was the most famous site of her worship. It was located on the Capitoline Hill in Rome. Minerva's shrine on the Aventine Hill in Rome was another meeting place for craftsmen. At one time it was used by dramatic poets and actors.

The Romans celebrated a festival to honor Minerva from March 19 through March 23. Known as the Quinquatria, it was widely accepted as a holiday for artists and students. Though her worship faded over time, Minerva remains an important part of Roman history. Her stories will be shared for years to come.

THE PARTHENON

The most famous temple dedicated to Minerva was the Parthenon. Located in Athens, Greece, this ancient temple was built between 447 and 432 BCE. It sat on a hill known as the Acropolis, where it overlooked the city. The ancient Greeks dedicated the temple to Athena because she was the patron goddess of their city. Ruins of the temple still remain today.

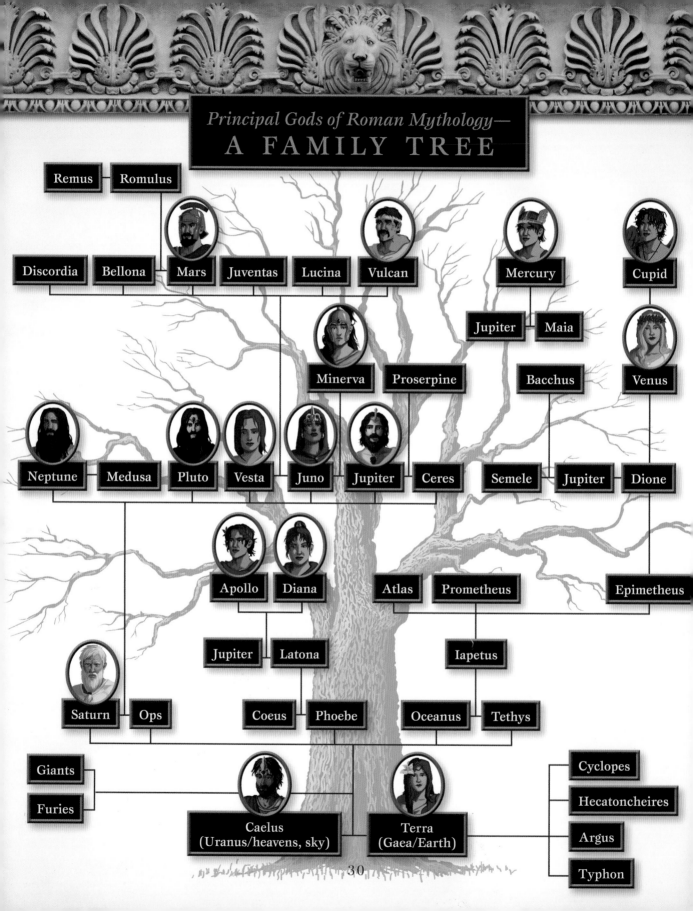

Principal Gods of Roman Mythology—
A FAMILY TREE

Remus — Romulus

Discordia — Bellona — Mars — Juventas — Lucina — Vulcan

Mercury

Cupid

Jupiter — Maia

Minerva — Proserpine

Bacchus

Venus

Neptune — Medusa — Pluto — Vesta — Juno — Jupiter — Ceres

Semele — Jupiter — Dione

Apollo — Diana

Atlas — Prometheus

Epimetheus

Jupiter — Latona

Iapetus

Saturn — Ops

Coeus — Phoebe

Oceanus — Tethys

Giants

Furies

Caelus
(Uranus/heavens, sky)

Terra
(Gaea/Earth)

Cyclopes

Hecatoncheires

Argus

Typhon

THE GREEK GODS

Ancient Greeks believed gods and goddesses ruled the world. The gods fell in love and struggled for power, but they never died. The ancient Greeks believed their gods were immortal. The Greek people worshiped the gods in temples. They felt the gods would protect and guide them. Over time, the Romans and many other cultures adopted the Greek myths as their own. While these other cultures changed the names of the gods, many of the stories remain the same.

SATURN: *Cronus*
God of Time and God of Sowing
Symbol: Sickle or Scythe

JUPITER: *Zeus*
King of the Gods, God of Sky, Rain, and Thunder
Symbols: Thunderbolt, Eagle, and Oak Tree

JUNO: *Hera*
Queen of the Gods, Goddess of Marriage,
*   Pregnancy, and Childbirth*
Symbols: Peacock, Cow, and Diadem
*   (Diamond Crown)*

NEPTUNE: *Poseidon*
God of the Sea
Symbols: Trident, Horse, and Dolphin

PLUTO: *Hades*
God of the Underworld
Symbols: Invisibility Helmet and Pomegranate

MINERVA: *Athena*
Goddess of Wisdom, War, and Arts and Crafts
Symbols: Owl, Shield, Loom, and Olive Tree

MARS: *Ares*
God of War
Symbols: Wild Boar, Vulture, and Dog

DIANA: *Artemis*
Goddess of the Moon and Hunt
Symbols: Deer, Moon, and Silver Bow and Arrows

APOLLO: *Apollo*
God of the Sun, Music, Healing, and Prophecy
Symbols: Laurel Tree, Lyre, Bow, and Raven

VENUS: *Aphrodite*
Goddess of Love and Beauty
Symbols: Dove, Swan, and Rose

CUPID: *Eros*
God of Love
Symbols: Bow and Arrows

MERCURY: *Hermes*
Messenger to the Gods, God of Travelers and Trade
Symbols: Crane, Caduceus, Winged Sandals,
*   and Helmet*

FURTHER INFORMATION

BOOKS

Mincks, Margaret. *What We Get from Roman Mythology.*
Ann Arbor, MI: Cherry Lake Publishing, 2015.

Temple, Teri. *Athena: Goddess of Wisdom, War, and Crafts.* Mankato, MN: Child's World, 2013.

Wolfson, Evelyn. *Mythology of the Romans.* Berkeley Heights, NJ: Enslow Publishers, 2014.

WEB SITES

Visit our Web site for links about Minerva: *childsworld.com/links*

Note to Parents, Teachers, and Librarians: We routinely verify our Web links to make sure they are safe and active sites. So encourage your readers to check them out!

INDEX